KT-170-450

THE WARLOCK'S STAFF

MINOS
THE DEMON BULL

With special thanks to
Allan Frewin Jones

To Connor Swift

www.beastquest.co.uk

ORCHARD BOOKS
338 Euston Road, London NW1 3BH
Orchard Books Australia
Level 17/207 Kent St, Sydney, NSW 2000

A Paperback Original
First published in Great Britain in 2011

Beast Quest is a registered trademark of Beast Quest Limited
Series created by Beast Quest Limited, London

Text © Beast Quest Limited 2011
Inside illustrations by Pulsar Estudio (Beehive Illustration)
Cover illustration by Steve Sims © Orchard Books 2011

A CIP catalogue record for this book is available from
the British Library.

ISBN 978 1 40831 317 6

Printed and bound in China by Imago

The paper and board used in this paperback are natural recyclable
products made from wood grown in sustainable forests. The
manufacturing processes conform to the environmental regulations of
the country of origin.

Orchard Books is a division of Hachette Children's Books,
an Hachette UK company

www.hachette.co.uk

Minos
THE DEMON BULL

BY ADAM BLADE

ORCHARD

Tom and Elenna are such fools! They thought their Quests were over and that my master was defeated. They were wrong! For now Malvel has the Warlock's Staff, hewn from the Tree of Being, and all kingdoms will soon be at his mercy.

We travel the land of Seraph, to find the Eternal Flame. And when we burn the Staff in the flame, our evil magic will be unstoppable. Tom and Elenna can chase us if they wish, but they'll find more than just Beasts lying in wait. They're alone this time, with no wizard to help them.

I hope Tom and Elenna are ready to meet me again. I've been waiting a long time for my revenge.

Yours, with glee, Petra the Witch

PROLOGUE

Jenka smiled as she brought the threshing flail down onto the grain. The chaff jumped. She loved to work alongside her mother as the sun smiled down on them.

Soon they would grind the wheat to make delicious flat-breads. She paused, resting her tired muscles.

Their grass hut was nearby, and in the wide fields beyond the village, cattle grazed contentedly under the perfectly blue and cloudless Seraph sky.

Her glance moved to the great totem pole that stood in the middle of the village. It had been hewn many years ago from the trunk of an ancient tree, its roots still deep in the ground. The pole was decorated with the faces of bulls and cows, carvings created in honour of the villges bountiful herds.

A moving figure caught her eye – a small cloaked shape gliding in from the pastures. It headed towards Minos, the most prized bull in the village. The figure stopped at the bull's stall and leant over the fence, holding out a cupped hand.

"Look, Mama," Jenka said, pointing to the cloaked figure. "A stranger is feeding Minos! Why aren't they afraid of him?"

Minos was a gentle creature, but

his size made most people wary. Her mother straightened her back and stared at the stranger.

"I don't know, Jenka," she said, "but you should go to them. Show them the hospitality of our people. Invite them to share our dinner. Go, child. I'll fetch our cooking pot."

As her mother moved towards their hut, Jenka ran along the path, passing the totem pole.

But as she came closer to the cloaked figure, she felt a chill run through her. The figure craned over the fence, holding out a palm.

Jenka hesitated, uneasy now as she watched Minos lower his head and lap at the food.

"Greetings," Jenka called. "My mother asks whether you'd like to share our midday meal. It's not much, but if you..."

Jenka's voice trailed away as the stranger turned and drew back her hood. A girl stared at her. She had a sly, cunning face framed in greasy dark hair. The girl's mouth twisted into a sneer.

"I won't be staying that long," she said. "It won't be safe around here soon!"

As Jenka recoiled from the cruel voice, the girl turned and hurried away, cackling to herself. Jenka saw some of the food scattered on the ground.

She crouched to look more carefully. The food looked like pine nuts, but they glowed with an other-worldly blue sheen.

"Magic?" Jenka muttered to herself. She was about to run and fetch her mother, when the fence rattled sharply. Looking up, Jenka saw that Minos had barged against the wooden barrier with his great horned head. Was he hungry for more of the strange food?

Jenka shivered with fear as she looked into the bull's eyes. They had taken on the blue colour of the seeds, and they shone brilliantly.

"Be still, Minos," Jenka called, her voice shaking as she backed away from the stall. "The girl has gone."

Jets of steam spurted from Minos's nostrils and he surged forwards again, snorting with sudden rage. This time the fence snapped like twigs under the force of his attack. Jenka stumbled away.

"Minos! All is well!" she cried in

fear. "Please, calm yourself!"

The bull lowered his horned head and began to rake his front hooves along the ground, preparing himself to charge.

A fearsome bellow broke from the Beast, as though he were in agony. Jenka watched in horror as the bull's body began to swell, his black hide stretching and expanding until Minos loomed above her. As he grew, his horns lengthened and thickened. Black claws sprouted from his hooves.

Jenka tried to cry for her mother – but no sound would come from her throat.

The bull's tail grew long and thick, lashing around a fence post like a whip and tearing it from the ground. With another bellow of

anger, Minos charged.

Jenka threw herself aside, her whole body shaken as the enraged beast pounded past, making for the village. She scrambled to her feet, dizzy and coughing on the dust that the bull's clawed hooves had kicked up.

Minos ploughed through the village, tearing fences apart, sending the other cattle stampeding for safety. Villagers fled in panic as the bull hurtled onwards.

Jenka let out a cry of anguish as she saw that the Beast was heading for her own hut. "Mother, get out!"

A moment later, the huge Beast plunged into the hut, smashing the woven grass walls, lifting his head to toss sheaves of the thatched roof high into the air. With a rush and a crash, the hut collapsed.

Jenka fell to her knees with a cry of despair.

Had Minos killed her mother?

CHAPTER ONE

THE TOUCH OF POISON

Tom and Elenna were riding along the edge of the forest. A gentle breeze made the leaves whisper and the branches dance. Elenna was sitting behind Tom on Storm's broad back, and Silver the wolf trotted along at their side.

Elenna was busy restringing her bow. She was using a string from the small

harp that Aduro had left for them,
along with five other magic tokens.

It wasn't long ago that the sweet
music of the harp had helped to
subdue Ursus, a Beast Malvel created.
Ursus had been a formidable enemy,
and Tom was weary from the battle,
but he knew that he would not have
a chance to rest and recover.

Tom knew that the wicked wizard,

Malvel, would be busy creating formidable new Beasts to throw at them.

But he was undaunted. "We have to stop him," he said to Elenna. "The fate of every kingdom depends on us."

Malvel and his loathsome minion, Petra, had stolen the Warlock's Staff from King Hugo's castle in Avantia. They meant to hurl the ancient staff into Seraph's Eternal Flame so that it would be burned to ash. If that happened, Malvel would have power over every kingdom, including Avantia.

"If we don't defeat Malvel, Aduro's death will have been for nothing," Elenna agreed.

It wrenched at Tom's heart to remember how the Good Wizard's clothes had crumpled to the ground as their old friend had vanished.

"But we do have Aduro's magical tokens to help us." Tom said. Tom patted Storm's saddlebag, where they were carefully stored: a leather harness decorated with metal studs and a green jewel, a phial, a chain mail vest, a knife and a jade whistle. Those tokens would help them to conquer whatever Beasts Malvel and Petra set against them, as long as Tom could work out what they did.

They had one other thing to aid them in Seraph. Petra, had dropped a map of the kingdom – a map that would lead Tom and Elenna to the Eternal Flame.

"All we have to do," Tom muttered, "is to defeat the Beasts that Malvel might put in our way." He took out the map and examined it.

"Does it still show the way forward?" Elenna asked, leaning around his shoulder to look.

"It does," said Tom. A gleaming silver thread traced its way down off the forested plateau of Seraph and into the wide plains. The glistening path came to a halt at a tiny picture of a bull.

"A bull Beast," Elenna said. "It will be strong."

Tom nodded. "And created by Malvel, who knows what it will be capable of?" he said. He rolled the linen scroll up and gazed down onto the plains. "We'd better get going. The sooner we find the Beast, the sooner we can free it."

After a while they came to the edge of the vast forest. A sudden wind rustled the leaves and sent the branches bending and swaying.

"I don't like the look of those clouds," said Elenna.

Great black clouds were rolling towards them at an alarming speed. The light faded as they quickly engulfed the sun. The air blew chilly in the sudden darkness.

"A storm is coming," agreed Tom. "A bad one."

The wind knifed up the hill and shrieked through the forest. Silver bared his teeth and growled. Storm rolled his eyes and flicked his ears back. The forest seemed to thrash and writhe against the fierce gale.

Tom looked grimly at Elenna. "Is it just me, or does this storm feel like the work of Malvel?"

Fat drops of rain began to fall,

splashing all around them and driving into their faces. Storm planted his hooves squarely on the ground, his head lowered against the unnatural weather.

"Should we shelter in the forest?" Elenna cried, her shoulders hunched and her face wet with rain.

Tom heard the creak and groan of a falling tree. High branches flailed. A mighty oak was crashing down towards them!

CHAPTER TWO

TORNADO

Storm neighed in fear as the huge tree toppled over towards them with a sickening creak. Tom gasped and jerked Storm's reins. His faithful horse stumbled away from the falling tree just as it crashed to the ground. A second later and they would have been crushed.

"That was too close. We need to keep clear of the forest,' Tom shouted. He gathered the reins and urged Storm to move towards the long slope that led down from the plateau. "We should try to find shelter on the plains."

"Silver!" Elenna called. "Keep close."

Cautiously, Tom guided Storm towards the hillside. The torrential rain pounded their faces, making it hard to see where they were going. Already, Tom's clothes were soaked and he was chilled to the bone.

Storm's hooves slithered in mud. Rivers of brown water were rushing all around them, turning the ground slick and slippery as ice. Elenna clung onto Tom as Storm fought to find a firm foothold.

Silver gave a howl as a blast of wind sent him tumbling.

Above the shriek of the wind, Tom
heard more trees crashing down in
the forest behind them. A heavy
branch came whirling through the
air, torn from some great forest tree.
It thudded to the ground close by,
quivering as it settled into the
thickening mudslide.

"We have to get further away from the forest!" Tom shouted. He peered ahead, desperately trying to spot some shelter. His eyes widened in alarm. Over the plains, the clouds were beginning to heave and swirl. Long probing fingers of black cloud came whirling down, stabbing at the land.

The screaming twisters lashed to and fro over the plains, moving across the ground as though searching for something.

For us? Tom wondered. Any one of those spiraling cones of wind could suck them up into the sky and tear them to pieces. But even as Tom watched, the twisters began to come together, joining up, growing and spinning, until they created a massive tornado.

The great tornado moved up the hill towards them. It towered over them, roaring and howling. More trees fell and massive branches were sucked up and flung aside like twigs.

Just when Tom felt sure the tornado would engulf them, it slowed and darkened, and through the whirl of black cloud a vast shape began to form.

"Malvel!" cried Tom, drawing his sword. "Just as I suspected."

The evil wizard had created an image of himself in the heart of the tornado.

"He's got the Warlock's Staff!" Elenna cried. Malvel's image bared its teeth in triumph, lifting the staff high. The wizard brandished it at them as lightning tore through the tornado, pulsing like blood, crackling

and snapping with blinding flashes
of white light.

The wizard's voice roared like
thunder. "Your Quest is futile," he
bellowed. "Look for the last time on
the Warlock's Staff, fools! I will burn
it in the Eternal Flame and all will
be lost."

"We'll never let that happen!" shouted Tom, his voice almost drowned out by the howl of the tornado and the crackle of lightning.

Malvel laughed till the ground shook. "Your pitiful friend Aduro is dead!" he taunted. "No one will be left to stop me from ruling Avantia and every other kingdom beyond. All your Quests – all your efforts – will have been in vain!"

Tom lifted his sword. "While there's blood in my veins I will fight you, Malvel!" he shouted. "I will not give in until the Staff is back in Avantia where it belongs and the kingdom of Seraph is safe from your evil!"

"Then I shall end your Quest now!" Malvel roared. Thunder crashed and a vicious shaft of lightning came hurtling straight towards them.

CHAPTER THREE

LIGHTNING STRIKES

Tom jerked on the reins and Storm made a stumbling move to the side. The spear of lightning struck the ground with a hissing sound and Silver howled, leaping for cover behind a rock. Steaming water spurted up, splashing hot on Tom's hands and face.

Undaunted, he pointed his sword

up defiantly into the heart of the whirling tornado. He could feel Elenna's hands holding on tightly around his waist. "One day I will destroy you!" he shouted against the roaring of the storm.

Malvel's huge face clouded with anger. He threw down more bolts of sizzling lightning. Tom and Elenna clung grimly to Storm's back as he leapt from side to side in the slippery mud to avoid being struck.

Snarling with rage, Malvel threw down shaft after shaft of lightning until the ground all around them was spitting and boiling like a cauldron.

I have to distract Malvel, Tom thought. *Storm can't avoid this lightning much longer.*

Clutching his sword and shield, Tom jumped from the saddle and ran across the hillside.

"Tom, what are you doing?" Elenna called.

"Creating a diversion!" Tom shouted back.

Malvel's lightning followed him, striking again and again in his footsteps, coming ever closer. Tom turned, lifting his shield. Just in time! A bolt of lightning struck off the wood, almost knocking Tom from his feet. He felt the fizz of energy

sparking through his body and his hair stood on end from the shock.

Elenna had also leapt down from Storm's back. She was fitting arrow after arrow to her bow, shooting up towards the tornado. But the wind was too fierce and her arrows were swept away before they could strike their target. Silver was at her side, snarling and jumping up, as if he wished to sink his teeth into Malvel.

How do I fight a tornado? Tom asked himself in desperation.

Another fork of lightning lashed down, blasting a deep hole in the ground. Tom scrambled away, but his muscles were weakening. He crouched, lifting his shield again. This time the bolt of bone-jarring lightning was deflected back up into the tornado. Malvel flinched as the lightning burned past him.

"I'll beat you yet!" Tom shouted.
"I'm a match for you, Malvel.
I always will be!"

The wizard shouted in anger and frustration. He brandished the Warlock's Staff as the tornado began to darken and whirl ever faster. What new peril was the wizard going to unleash?

The whipping tail of the tornado lifted into the air like the black sting of some monstrous insect. Then it lashed down, thrusting into the ground at Tom's feet and sending stones and earth exploding in every direction.

Tom lifted his shield, feeling the hammering of stones on its face.

A second time the tornado's end flicked across the ground, gouging

out a deep steep-sided hollow. If Tom
fell into one of these craters, he'd be
unable to escape.

"Back!" Tom shouted to his friends.
"Try to get back to the forest!" As he
turned, he noticed a shadowy figure
darting behind a rock, not far from
Storm, but he had no time to wonder
who it could be.

"We're coming!" Elenna shouted.

"Go ahead! We're right behind you!"

Tom zigzagged towards the trees. He glanced over his shoulder, seeing the tornado spinning around, filling the dark sky, howling like a thousand demons. Malvel's eyes gleamed with hatred as the narrow base of the tornado whipped through the rain-filled air and came crashing into the hillside at Tom's feet.

The blast loosened the earth and Tom saw a landslide slithering down in front of him. He teetered on the edge of the gouged-out hollow. But even as he fought for balance, Storm came too close, unable to find solid ground under his hooves. The ground gave way and both Tom and his horse toppled over the edge.

CHAPTER FOUR

HUNTING THE THIEF

Tom let out a cry of anguish as he clung to the rocky edge. Storm slid down in a flurry of mud.

Malvel's laughter roared in his ears.

Then a voice called down. "Tom! Give me your hand!"

Elenna was above him on solid ground, Silver at her side. Tom reached up and grasped her hand, but no sooner had he begun to clamber up than the ridge of land under her feet broke loose. With the storm screaming in their heads, Tom and his companions went sliding helplessly down the mudslide.

As he plunged into the muddy chasm, Tom heard the crack and groan of falling trees all around him. Malvel's blast had torn several huge trees out of the ground, and they were tumbling down the slope in their wake.

Tom struck a hard shoulder of rock and crashed to a breathless halt in thick rain-spattered mud. He lay gasping for a moment, too bruised and battered to move. He opened his eyes and saw branches plummeting towards him. Instinctively, he thrust his shield upwards as the tree thumped down. Branches closed over him like a cage.

The noise stopped and an eerie silence descended. Even the rain had ceased. Tom struggled to his feet and cut his way free of the branches.

"Elenna!" he cried, afraid that his friends had been injured. "Elenna! Silver! Storm!"

A low moaning reached his ears. He turned, hacking through the debris of the fallen trees, his feet slithering in the mud. He saw Elenna's legs sticking out from under a branch.

"Keep still," he called to her. "I'll get you free." He heaved the branch up and dragged it aside. Gasping for breath, he saw Elenna's dirt-smeared face looking up at him in relief.

"Are you hurt?" Tom asked, helping her to her feet.

"No, I don't think so. But what about Silver and Storm?"

From close by, they heard a snorting and whinnying noise. Looking dirty and bedraggled, Storm came walking slowly towards them, and Silver was at his side, muddy and wet, but unharmed.

"Everyone is safe!" said Tom, gripping his sword. "Now for Malvel!"

"I think he's gone," said Elenna.

As Tom gazed upwards, he saw that the tornado had vanished. The storm clouds were clearing away as quickly as they'd arrived. Within moments, the sun shone brightly again in the peaceful blue sky of Seraph.

"He must think he finished us off," Tom said with a grim smile. "He's underestimated us." He sheathed his sword. "We'll make him regret that."

"Let's clean ourselves off first,' said Elenna. "We're filthy."

"Good idea," said Tom.

Silver howled and went bounding away to where a pool of clear rainwater lay in a hollow in the grass. Tom, Elenna and Storm

followed the wolf as he rolled
in the shallow pool.

It didn't take long to get the filth
off, and soon even Storm was looking
like his old self.

"Now we have to get going!" said
Tom, lifting a foot to climb into the
saddle. But he paused. "Where's the
saddlebag?" Sure enough, the bag
with the five tokens in it was missing.

"It must have been torn off in the
fall," said Elenna. "Yes!" she
exclaimed, running forwards and
pulling the bag out of a pool of mud.
"It's here!" She held the bag up.
"The tokens have fallen out," she
said. "Where are they?"

Tom took the bag from Elenna.
There was a neat line in the bottom
of the bag. *That's no tear*, he thought,
remembering the shadowy figure

he'd seen flitting behind rocks.
"Someone's cut the bag open. While
we were fighting Malvel, she stole
the tokens!"

Elenna's eyes widened. "Petra!"

Tom nodded. He looked into
Elenna's worried eyes. "We have to
get them back," he said.

"Silver can help," his friend
suggested. She called the wolf over
and held the bag to his nose. "Take
a good sniff, boy," she said, stroking
his head. "Can you smell something
witchy?"

Silver sniffed, his eyes glittering.
He lifted his head and barked sharply.
Moments later, he was racing along,
low to the ground.

"Mount up," Tom called to Elenna.
"We don't want to lose him."

They rode Storm out of the valley,

and onto the lush plains. Silver was moving quickly through the long grass.

Tom lifted his eyes from the wolf for a moment. The plains of Seraph seemed to stretch on forever under the sun, and already his clothing was drying off.

We should be tracking down the Beast, Tom thought in frustration. *But we had to get those tokens back first.*

They came to a narrow earthy path, winding its way through grasses so tall that they came up to Storm's shoulders. Silver's tail whisked around a bend ahead of them. He gave a bark as if to tell them to keep up.

"Look," said Elenna, pointing down at a series of prints in the earth. They were the indentations of shoes. Someone was running ahead of them.

"These were made recently," said Tom. "I think we're getting close to our little thief."

They rode around the bend. Silver was loping along a long straight stretch of the path – and some distance ahead, moving quickly, was a hooded and cloaked figure.

"Shoot a warning arrow over

her head, Elenna," suggested Tom. "Let her know she can't get away from us now."

Elenna fitted an arrow to her bow. She aimed carefully and let loose with a twang. The arrow arched over Silver's back, then dipped and came thudding into the path a pace ahead of the fleeing figure.

The figure leapt to one side with a shriek of fear.

"Silver! Hold back!" Tom called, urging Storm into a gallop. "I have her!"

He rode past the panting wolf and jumped down from the saddle, drawing his sword as he confronted the cowering figure.

"Now, Petra, you thief!" he shouted, pointing his sword towards her. "Give me back those tokens!"

The figure fell to her knees. "No!" she wailed, holding her clasped hands out towards him. "Please don't kill me!"

Tom lifted his sword, ready to defend himself against the witch before she could cast a spell on him. But at that moment, the hood fell back to reveal the terrified face of a girl he had never seen before.

CHAPTER FIVE

THE RUINED VILLAGE

"I'm sorry," Tom said, sheathing his sword. "I won't harm you. I thought you were someone else." Ashamed to have frightened the girl, he held out a friendly hand.

She got shakily to her feet, her eyes still anxious and she darted glances at the others as they approached.

Tom saw the missing tokens

clutched in a fold of the girl's cloak.
So, she *was* the thief.

"Why did you steal from us?" he
asked gently.

"I was so hungry," she groaned.
"I saw the sack tied to the horse, and
I thought the rider must have been
killed in the storm. I was looking for
food, but when I saw these... Well,
I thought we might be able to sell
them." She opened the cloak and he
took the tokens. Tears were running
down the girl's face.

Smiling, Tom held out a clenched
fist, palm down. He had learnt that
this was a sign of peace and greeting
in Seraph.

Blinking her tears away, the girl
returned the gesture. They touched
knuckles.

"Tell us what happened to you,"

Tom asked as Elenna dismounted and came up to them. Silver was close by. The girl flinched as the wolf sniffed at her.

"Don't be frightened," Elenna said. "Silver would never harm you."

"My name is Jenka," the girl said at last. "I live in a village with my mother. We herd our cattle and do no one any harm." Her voice caught in her throat. Elenna rested a hand on her shoulder. Silver sniffed her hand and the girl smiled and stroked his fur.

"Go on," Elenna said.

"Things went wrong when a young woman came to our village and fed some evil seeds to our prize bull, Minos," Jenka continued. "The food turned Minos into…into a terrible wild monster."

Tom and Elenna glanced at one another. Jenka was talking about a Beast!

"He attacked the village and destroyed my home." Fresh tears came. "My mother is still trapped in the ruins of our house. Everyone else has fled. I'm not strong enough to free her – I've been keeping her alive by dropping scraps of food to her." Her voice rose to a wail. "But I have no more food to give her! She'll die!"

"No," Tom said firmly. "She won't. Come on – get onto Storm's back. Show us the way to your village."

"Now we'll get to the Beast at last," he whispered to Elenna. She nodded in agreement. Tom allowed the two girls to mount up while he jogged alongside with Silver close behind.

It didn't take them long to reach

the village. Many of the fences had been ripped up, and nearly half of the grass huts were smashed and trampled. A tall trunk of wood stood in the middle of the village, topped with the carving of a bull's head.

"That's our totem pole," Jenka explained. "The bull is sacred to us. We rely on our cattle to give us everything we need. Now the herd has run away." She gazed nervously around the half-ruined village. There was no sign of the Beast. "Minos may return at any moment," Jenka mumbled. "We're not safe here."

"Which is your house?" asked Elenna.

Jenka jumped down from Storm's back and ran to a crushed hut close to the centre of the village. "Mother?" she called. "I'm back! I've brought help."

Tom ran to the hut in time to hear a weak voice reply.

"Bless you, my child."

"I'll get you free," Tom called determinedly. He had already witnessed the death of his great friend Aduro – he was not going to stand by and let another person die. "How are you trapped?"

"The central roof beam has fallen across my legs," called the pain-wracked voice. "I can't lift it."

"Wait a moment," Tom called. He ran back to Storm and drew down the rope that was looped around the pommel of his saddle. Returning to the crushed hut, he clambered carefully in among the remains of the fallen roof until he found a small gap.

"Are you there?" he called.

A pale hand lifted in response.

"Take the rope and tie it to the beam," Tom instructed the trapped woman.

The bruised fingers caught hold of the rope and pulled it down.

Tom climbed out of the wreckage and fed the rope out. Then he tied the end to Storm's saddle.

"Pull with all your might, boy!" Tom urged Storm. The noble stallion turned and walked away. The rope became taut and Tom and Elenna went to his bridle, encouraging him to pull harder.

There was a creak and a groan and a rush of sliding grass as Storm dragged the beam away from the house.

Tom and Jenka ran forwards and helped the slim woman climb out of the wreckage. Pieces of straw were caught in her tangled hair and her gown was torn. There were cuts and bruises on her face and arms, but she did not seem to have been seriously hurt. Tom stepped back as Jenka and

her mother hugged in relief. Tom saw
the woman wince. She was holding
her hand awkwardly.

"Have you been injured?" Tom
asked.

"I think I may have broken my
fingers," the woman said, wincing in
pain. Jenka looked anxiously at her
with tears in her eyes.

"Mama, no!" she cried.

"I can heal your mother," Tom said. He took the green jewel of Skor from his belt and pressed it gently against the woman's hand. Tom had won this jewel on a previous Quest, and it had the power to heal.

Jenka's mother gasped. "The pain is gone," she said, her eyes wide in wonder. "Thank you."

Smiling, Tom picked the talon of Epos from his shield and ran it over the woman's cuts and bruises. In a few moments they had all disappeared.

"I cannot thank you enough for this," the woman gasped. But her words faded away as the ground beneath their feet began to shake.

"Is it an earthquake?" asked Elenna. A growl from Silver made them all turn. A shape stood on the horizon, as black a night, as huge as one of the huts.

A dreadful reverberating bellow shook the air.

"Minos!" cried Jenka. "He's returned to kill us!"

The monstrous bull lifted his head; his evil eyes glaring, his huge horns glinting wickedly in the sunlight, nostrils snorting black steam. The bull's long tail lashed to and fro and its massive hooves pawed the ground, the long black claws gouging out heavy clods of earth.

Before Tom had the chance to move, the bull lowered its head and charged towards them.

CHAPTER SIX

HORNS OF DEATH

"Run!" cried Jenka, tugging at her mother's arm as the Beast thundered towards them.

Tom stepped in front of Jenka and her mother. "Find shelter," he told them.

The ground quivered as the huge Beast charged into the village, kicking up great clouds of dust. Tom spread his feet, his sword and shield ready, his eyes firmly fixed on the snorting monster. "Elenna," he said. "Get everyone to safety. Make sure Storm and Silver are with you."

"Stay there," he heard Elenna say as she led them all behind one of the huts that was still standing. She sprang onto Storm's back and from there she climbed onto the roof. She knelt on the thatch, fitting an arrow to her bow.

Tom prepared himself for battle as Minos came hurtling towards him. There was a deadly blue gleam in the Beast's mad eyes, and the wicked tips of his massive horns looked sharp enough to pierce right through Tom's shield.

As the Beast pounded closer, Elenna shot arrows at him, but the shafts bounced off the thick hide.

It would take more than arrows to
stop Minos.

A sudden thought struck Tom.
Sheathing his sword, he spun and
snatched up a panel of the woven
grass wall of the fallen hut. Holding it
in front of him like a second shield,
he crouched, his muscles as tense as

the string of Elenna's bow.

The whole world seemed to shake as the bull charged at him. He had to time this exactly right.

Above the ear-splitting hammering of the hooves, Tom could hear Jenka crying out in fright.

The bull was almost upon him, but he held his ground. "Do your worst!" he shouted. At the very last second, Tom sprang aside, whisking the grass shield away a moment before the great blunt head would have smashed into it.

Minos went careering past, snorting black steam as he crashed into the remains of the ruined hut. His hooves tangled with the woven grass and he came to a slow halt. His great sides heaved as he breathed, his head turning, the blue eyes filled with anger and malice as he stared at Tom.

The Beast's long vicious claws gouged the ground, sending clumps of earth flying. He turned, lifting his head and opening his wide red mouth in a ferocious and deafening roar.

"I'm not so easy to trample as a hut, because huts don't move!" Tom taunted, brandishing the shield of grass in front of him. "Try again, you lumbering brute! Catch me if you can!"

Tom winced as Minos let out an ear-splitting roar of rage. The clawed hooves raked the ground, the mighty head lowered and the Beast charged again, the good creature driven to madness and confusion by Malvel's spell.

Tom held the grass shield steady,

judging the right moment for
a second time.

As Minos rampaged towards him,
Tom leapt high, dropping his grass
shield as he sprang over the Beast's
head. Minos's horns caught in the
weave of the grass, blinding him for
a few moments.

Tom landed feet first on the Beast's
muscular neck. Spreading his arms,
he ran swiftly up onto the bull's high
hump and along its spine. Realizing
that his prey had escaped
a second time, Minos shuddered to
a halt, shaking his shoulders to try
and dislodge Tom from his back.

Tom leapt sideways, avoiding the
lashing whip of the tail. He
somersaulted in the air and came
to a rolling landing.

"Well done, Tom!" Elenna cried.

But the deadly Beast was quicker on his feet than Tom had expected. The spikes that stuck out from his massive hooves seemed to give him the power to turn in an instant. Tom was still getting to his feet as he saw the Beast pounding towards him for a third time.

Tom threw himself aside, but the tip of one of the Beast's horns clipped his shield and he was sent spinning to the ground. A fierce pain exploded in his head as he crashed to earth with bone-jarring force.

He lay gasping for a moment, drawing his sword and gathering his strength. But while he was still recovering, the Beast attacked again.

Tom turned onto his back, holding his shield up, ready to stab with his sword. The Beast reared over him like a black mountain. Foul-smelling breath billowed from the huge nostrils and slimy spittle rained down from the curling lips.

A hoof lifted high, ready to crush Tom into the ground. But before it could be brought down, Tom heard a ferocious howling. He saw from the corner of his eye a grey shape speeding through the air.

Silver! The brave wolf fell on the Beast's huge neck, his fangs sinking into the thick black hide, his claws scrabbling. But the bull tossed its head and Silver was thrown off. Tom watched in dismay as his loyal friend was flung through the air with a drawn-out howl. Silver went skidding to the ground, tumbling over and over, whining in pain.

Minos's hoof came crashing down

like a great hammer, and Tom only
just had time to roll out of the way.

Tom leapt to his feet. Minos's horns
swept around and Tom had to jump
high into the air to avoid being
scythed down. Again the Beast's head
turned, and this time Tom snatched
at the horn, catching hold of it and

using it to lift himself into the air.
He swung high, but Minos flicked his
massive head, loosening Tom's grip
on the horn and he fell awkwardly
onto his knees beside the bull.

"Watch out for the tail!" he heard
Elenna shout.

Even as he scrambled up, the long
tail snapped towards him. It curled
around his ankles like a noose,
drawing tight and pulling Tom's feet
out from under him.

With a gasp, Tom fell headlong as

the tail drew his feet together,
making it impossible for him to
get up.

And then, roaring with anger, the
great Beast lumbered away, dragging
Tom helplessly behind him over the
hard and bumpy ground.

CHAPTER SEVEN

THE ENEMY FROM THE SKY

Tom felt as though his bones were being shaken loose in his body as the rampaging Beast hauled him along. He managed to keep hold of his sword and shield as he grabbed at broken fence posts, but the Beast's speed snatched his hands away.

He heard the whiz of arrows and saw that Elenna was shooting shaft

after shaft at the Beast. But the
arrows only snapped or bounced
off the monster's tough hide.

At last, Tom was dragged to a
stretch of grassy ground. He had
a moment or two to gather his wits.
He clenched his fist tightly around
the hilt of his sword and brought its
blade down with all his strength on
the tail. Minos bellowed in pain as
the sword cut through. Now free,

Tom rolled over and over in the long grass, his ears filled with the bellows of the Beast.

Dazed and battered, Tom forced himself to his feet, ignoring the pain and dizziness. He had injured the Beast – perhaps if he could get close enough to shear off some of those claws, he would bring Minos to his knees.

But the injured Beast did not turn

on him. Roaring in fury, it charged away across the fields.

"Tom, are you all right?" called Elenna, running towards him. Silver was at her side, howling and snarling, unhurt despite his brave attack on the Beast.

"I survived!" gasped Tom, stooping to untangle the loops of the tail from around his ankles. "But I don't think we've ever met a more dangerous Beast." He looked over to where Storm stood with Jenka and her mother. "I don't even know which of the tokens we'll need to defeat it. It could be the whistle, or the chainmail vest or the phial."

"Tom! Look! Minos has stopped," Elenna warned.

Sure enough, the great black monster had halted out in the fields.

The Beast stared unblinking back at the village. His clawed hooves scored the ground and he lifted his head. A roar echoed through the air.

Tom touched the ruby jewel on his belt. Perhaps with the aid of Torgor's ruby, he would be able to communicate with the enraged Beast.

He stepped over to the smashed fence of Minos's paddock and picked up a coil of rope with a loop at one end. "I'm going to try to make the Beast understand me," he said. "If I can calm him down I may be able to get this rope around his neck." He looked uneasily at Elenna. "I don't know if this is going to work."

"Maybe not," Elenna said. "But I think it might be your only option."

Tom walked into the field with Elenna only a few paces behind him.

"Minos, I know you're a good animal under an evil spell," Tom called, moving forwards through the grass. "I don't want to fight you." The bull tossed his horns and snorted black smoke.

"You have been changed by an evil wizard," Tom continued, still moving cautiously forwards. "He is using you to harm us and to harm all of Seraph."

Minos stopped clawing the ground. His sides shook as he snorted, but his eyes seemed to lose some of their anger and fire.

"It's working," breathed Elenna. "Even if he doesn't fully understand. Tom, you're calming him."

But would Minos allow Tom to put the rope around his neck?

He was only a few steps from the

Beast now, and still Minos did not attack. Tom and the Beast stared into one another's eyes. The evil blue glint faded. The Beast was quite calm now. Only two more paces forwards and Tom would be able to place a hand on Minos's great neck.

A sudden shape in the sky caught Tom's eye. For a moment, he couldn't make out what it was, but as it raced down the sky and came closer, he recognized Petra the witch, seated astride her winged black unicorn. The unicorn neighed as its wings beat, its lips curling back to reveal yellow fangs.

As swift as lightning, Elenna loosed her arrows into the air, but Petra was too agile to be stopped that easily. Cackling with glee, she jerked the reins from side to side, steering the unicorn in a zigzag course as the shafts sped uselessly past.

"Did you really think my Beast could be defeated by your simple mind tricks?" she howled down at Tom. "It will take more than that to beat me and my master!"

She unfurled a long whip. The unicorn flew low over the Beast and Petra lashed Minos viciously across his back. "Kill him, my beauty!" she howled. "Trample him into the ground!"

The Beast bellowed in anger and pain, the blue light igniting in his eyes again.

"No!" gasped Tom, falling back. "Minos – don't let her do this to you!"

But it was too late. Malvel's evil magic coursed through the bull's blood.

Leaping backwards, Tom lifted his shield to fend off the Beast's attack. But his footing wasn't firm enough and he was thrown to the ground as Mino's forehead struck against his shield like a battering ram.

CHAPTER EIGHT

BRAINS AGAINST BRAWN

Tom rolled over and over as the spikes tore his clothing and the great hooves pounded down all around him. Using all his strength, he hammered the rim of his shield into one of Minos's forelegs. Bellowing in pain, the Beast backed away for a moment and at last Tom was able to scramble clear.

He sprang up, sword and shield at the ready. He saw Elenna racing over to where Silver was lying, still dazed from his attack on the Beast. Storm had come out of hiding and was standing protectively in front of Jenka and her mother.

Careering to a halt, Minos turned and lunged at Tom with his horns. Tom fended off the blow with his shield, bringing his sword down onto the horn with a ringing crash.

Sparks flew up as Tom's blade glanced off the tough surface of the horn.

I don't want to kill the Beast if I can help it, he thought. *But I must defeat it to break the spell.*

Step by step, the enraged Beast drove Tom back.

Then, with a final bellow, the Beast

turned away from Tom. Steam
snorted from Minos's nostrils and
blue fire flickered in his enraged eyes
as he charged across the village,
destroying more of the huts.

Elenna ran up to Tom, Silver at her
side. "The Beast won't stop until the
entire village is ruined," she gasped.

Tom nodded. "And unless I defeat
him, he'll run wild through the
whole kingdom!" Fired by a new
determination, Tom ran after the

rampaging Beast. He vaulted through the debris of crushed huts, calling on the piece of Tagus's horseshoe attached to his shield to give him the speed to catch up with Minos.

"Minos!" Tom shouted as he closed in on the Beast. "Turn and fight me if you dare!"

Minos came to a halt, dust rising all about him as he turned to stare at Tom. Already several more huts lay ruined in his wake. Steam snorted from his nostrils and blue fire flickered in his enraged eyes.

Tom beat his sword on his shield to keep the Beast's attention.

I'll never defeat him in a head-on fight, Tom thought.

But there was one hope. Tom remembered the way the people of Errinel would tame horses out on the plains by leaping aboard their backs and riding them until there was no fight left in them.

But would that even be possible with Minos?

"I have to try," Tom muttered under his breath. "It's my only hope. But I'll have to take him by surprise."

Feigning weakness, he staggered back from the Beast, lowering his sword and shield as though he was exhausted. Roaring, the Beast came charging at him. At the last moment, Tom brought his shield around with all his might and struck the Beast on the muzzle.

Startled by the sudden blow, Minos reared back, snorting and shaking his huge head.

I need to be able to control the Beast, Tom thought. *And only one of the tokens will help me stay on his back.*

"Throw me the harness from the bag of tokens!" he shouted to Elenna.

She dug her arm into the sack – Jenka's mother had mended it for them.

Minos charged, taking Tom by surprise and crashing into him with his huge forehead. Tom was thrown backwards. He struck Elenna and the two of them tumbled into the ruins of a hut.

Elenna struggled to get to her feet.

"No!" Tom whispered. "Keep down. Let him think we're defeated. But give me the harness."

Elenna passed the magic harness to him then lay still among the broken grass walls. The leather of the harness felt soft and supple in his hands. At its centre was a green jewel and some of

the leather was decorated with metal
studs. Just holding the harness made
his skin tingle.

To his alarm, Tom heard Jenka and
her mother shouting as they ran
forwards to come to their aid.

This would ruin his plan!

He pushed up through the debris
of the grass wall. "No!" he called to
them. "Get away!"

But it was too late. Tom saw Minos
turn his heavy head. Drool dripped as

he opened his mouth wide in a bellow of rage. Turning his huge bulk away from Tom, the Beast churned up the ground with his clawed hooves then lowered his head and charged at Jenka and her mother.

Jenka's mother snatched at Jenka's arm and pulled her back. They were running fast, but Tom knew how quickly the Beast would catch them.

Maybe I can still make this work, Tom thought.

He sprang to his feet. "Minos! I'm still alive!" he shouted. "Come and fight me again, if you dare!"

But the charging bull ignored his challenge. Tom called to Storm. "Here, boy! Quickly!"

In a moment Tom was in the saddle and galloping after the Beast. As they closed in, Tom saw the severed length of Minos's tail lying coiled on the ground. Hanging half out of the saddle, he snatched it up.

"Faster, Storm!" Tom urged. "Faster!"

The bull hurtled through a ruined hut, tossing sheaves of grass into the air and grinding the walls to shreds under his hooves. Tom could see that Minos was too fast for Jenka and her fleeing mother. A few moments more and he would trample them to death.

But Storm had almost caught up with him. Tom dug his heels into Storm's flanks and the stallion responded with a final surge that brought them up alongside the rampaging Beast.

Tom knew that he had only one chance to save them. Swinging the tail over his head like a lasso, he threw it forwards. Luck was with him; the end

of the tail wound around and around
one of Minos's horns.

"Storm, stop!" Tom shouted,
tugging on the reins. The stallion
drew up sharply. Tom yanked on
the tail, pulling Minos's head to one
side. Jenka and her mother were
still running, looking back, their

faces wild with fear.

The Beast stumbled and came crashing down in a cloud of dust as Storm leapt over him, avoiding the flailing hooves. "Keep running!" Tom called to Jenka and her mother. "Find somewhere to hide."

Tom knew Minos would not stay down for long. But even he was surprised by the speed with which the mighty Beast rocked to his feet again. Minos turned on him, shaking his horns with fury.

Tom had rescued Jenka and her mother from certain death, but now Minos was more enraged than ever. As the Beast charged, Storm reared up in panic, throwing Tom to the ground.

Tom lay gasping and defenseless as Minos bore down on him.

CHAPTER NINE

RIDING THE BEAST

Tom hurled himself aside as the mighty Beast thundered past. His only hope of harnessing Minos would be to distract him first. But how?

Petra had come upon the Beast from above when she had attacked him – perhaps that was the answer. Tom glanced up at the totem pole, a dangerous plan forming in his head.

The Beast rampaged across the

village, turning in a wide circle, ready to come at Tom again. Elenna was close by, an arrow on the string.

"Elenna! Mount Storm!" he shouted to her. "Try to make the Beast follow you – but don't get too far ahead of him."

Nodding, Elenna jumped into Storm's saddle. She snatched up the bridle and urged Storm to a rapid canter, guiding the brave horse across the path of Minos's enraged charge.

The Beast's eyes gleamed as he saw this new target for his wrath. He turned aside, hurtling after Elenna and Storm. Gripping with her knees, Elenna twisted in the saddle and fired an arrow at the Beast. It glanced off his horn, and he gave a bellow of rage and gathered speed.

"Faster, Storm!" Elenna cried.

The stallion galloped across the village with the Beast in pursuit.

Tom ran to the totem pole and began to climb with the glowing harness hanging over his shoulder. Climbing quickly, Tom came to the summit of the totem pole. The wrecked village spread out beneath him – he could see Jenka and her mother crouching behind a smashed hut with Silver standing protectively by them.

Tom put his fingers to his lips and let out a shrill whistle. "Come this way!"

Elenna nodded and flicked the reins, bringing Storm around in a tight curve so he galloped towards the totem pole with the Beast close behind.

Tom had to judge this perfectly!

As Minos thundered past the pole,
Tom leapt off. He landed high on the
mighty bull's back, feeling the
muscles of the thick neck bunching
between his legs. The ridges of the
Beast's spine were sharp and hard
under him and the foul stench of
Minos's hide filled his nostrils.

He almost slid from the Beast's neck, but he managed to cling to a tuft of the bull's hair to prevent himself from falling.

The Beast bucked and reared, snorting and bellowing as he lurched from side to side in an effort to hurl Tom from his back. Shaken to his bones, Tom hung grimly on.

You won't throw me off that easily, he thought.

His every muscle and sinew straining, Tom edged down towards the bull's thick neck. He slipped the harness off his shoulder. Clinging on to the Beast's hair with one hand, Tom slung the harness forwards, the green jewel glinting in the light. But the studded harness slid uselessly off the side of Minos's head. Gritting his teeth with the effort, Tom threw

again. Luck was with him this time!
The harness fell into place over
Minos's head.

The maddened Beast tossed his
horns, furiously trying to get free.
Tom held on tight – but now he had
to subdue the Beast. He struggled to
draw his sword. He didn't intend to
kill Minos, but he hoped to bring the
hilt down between the wide horns
and stun him.

The Beast twisted his head and one
horn caught Tom's sword and sent it
spinning out of his grip. Minos
fought even more ferociously to hurl
Tom off. Tom lurched wildly, clinging
on with both hands, only just
managing to stay in place as the
leather thongs of the harness bit
deep into his skin.

Bellowing, the Beast went racing

across the fields and it was all Tom could do not to be thrown to the ground.

If the harness doesn't work, I'll never be able to defeat Minos and break Malvel's enchantment, he thought desperately.

But as Minos thundered on, it seemed to Tom that the Beast's rage was gradually ebbing away. He was slowing down and the bellowing was not so ferocious. The magical token was working! Tom knew he had to act now, before the Beast freed himself from the harness.

Gripping the straps in one fist, Tom pulled his shield from his back. He brought its edge down sharply between the Beast's horns. Minos roared in anger, but Tom's blow wasn't powerful enough to knock the monster out.

The Beast ran in a circle, and headed back to the village. Tom saw the totem pole ahead. He edged down the powerful neck to the horns. Letting go of the leather thongs of the harness, he grasped the horns in both hands. He took a deep breath, preparing himself for a final effort.

Releasing both hands, he threw himself forward over the horns, twisting in midair and grabbing the horns again. He stamped his feet against the Beast's huge muscular shoulders, facing Minos now and holding a horn in each hand.

He was hanging in front of the

Beast's face and the black steam from
Minos's nostrils blasted all around
him, its foul smell making him
choke. The dreadful blue eyes
stared at him in fury.

His fingers burned with the strain
and he knew he couldn't hold this
position for long. He glanced over his
shoulder. They were nearing the
totem pole. Using every ounce of his
remaining strength, Tom wrenched
on the horns, turning the Beast's
head and forcing him to twist to
one side.

He flicked another glance over his
shoulder. The Beast was thundering
directly towards the pole at full
speed.

"Tom!" he heard Elenna's fearful
voice above the roaring of the Beast
and the hammering of his hooves.

"Tom, you'll be killed!"

Tom glanced over his shoulder again. They were almost upon the totem pole. Now he had to act with speed and precision. If he got this wrong, he'd die.

CHAPTER TEN

THE LAST HOPE

At the last possible moment, Tom managed to hurl himself aside as Minos crashed into the totem pole. He heard a loud crack and then a sudden silence.

Tom struck the ground with an agonizing thump. Every muscle hurting, he sprawled in the dirt, coughing and choking.

Staggering to his feet, Tom saw that

the totem pole had been split open by
the impact. Minos lay on his side at
the foot of the totem pole. His flanks
rose and fell rapidly as he breathed,
but the collision had stunned the
Beast. Tom could see the harness's
green jewel glowing more brightly
now as Aduro's magic grew stronger.

Nursing his bruised and aching

limbs, Tom limped cautiously towards the Beast.

Elenna brought Storm to a halt and jumped down, running to Tom's side with Silver loping along behind her.

"Is it over?" she asked unsurely.

"I think so," said Tom. He pointed to the clouds that still blew from the bull's nostrils. "See that? The steam is white now, not black."

Elenna came closer to Minos's head. She knelt and cautiously lifted one of the bull's eyelids. "His eyes aren't blue anymore," she said. "I think the enchantment has worn off!"

As Tom and Elenna watched, the Beast's gigantic body began to shrink. The long black claws withered away to nothing on the hooves and the massive horns dwindled down to their usual size. Within the space of ten heartbeats, Minos had turned back into a normal bull.

Minos lifted his head and blew steam, staring at Tom and Elenna with a confused look in his gentle brown eyes.

Tom took hold of the harness and helped the bull get to his feet. Minos stood in front of them, still huge but quiet and gentle, quivering a little and shaking his head as though ridding himself of the last remnants of Petra's evil magic.

Tom gently slid the magical harness off the bull's head. The jewel had stopped glowing now, Tom noticed. It had fulfilled its role.

Jenka and her mother ran over with Silver at their sides.

"Jenka, be careful," her mother warned.

"No, mother – look," Jenka cried, pressing her face to the bull's neck and stroking his muzzle. "He's better now!" She looked at Tom and Elenna with shining eyes. "Thank you so much."

Minos allowed himself to be petted for a few moments then stepped away from Jenka and turned to face the fields. He lifted his head and let out a great bellow.

"What's he doing?" asked Elenna.

"You'll see," said Jenka's mother. A few moments later, dozens of large dark shapes appeared on the horizon. Tom realized they were cows, and other bulls.

"The villagers' cattle are coming back," he gasped.

Following them were the villagers – herdsmen and women in simple clothing with their children trotting along at their sides, returning to their homes now that everything had been made safe again. Tom saw relief on many faces, but there were tears and looks of dismay, too, as the people saw the devastation that the Beast had caused.

Soon, Tom and Elenna were surrounded by people asking what had happened to Minos to make him so violent. Tom explained his Quest and the villagers listened, enthralled.

A woman took Elenna by the hands. "Thank you," she said, her eyes brimming with tears.

"We will never forget your bravery," said a man, resting his hand on Tom's shoulder.

"You must stay here for the night," Jenka's mother said. "We'll prepare an evening meal for you – it is the least we can do after all that you have risked to help us."

"It's a kind offer," Tom said, "but we can't afford the time to rest. We have to find the evil people who enchanted Minos, and we have to stop them causing even more damage in Seraph."

"We must press on and find the Eternal Flame," Elenna said.

Tom and Elenna mounted Storm and Silver stood ready at their side. They were about to leave when Jenka's mother handed them a bag. "Take this at least," she said. "For your journey." Tom opened the bag. It contained bread rolls and cheese in a cloth wrap, along with some apples.

"Thank you," he said, glad to accept the gift.

"Good luck on your journey," said

Jenka's mother, and the other
villagers gathered around, also
calling out, "Good luck! Farewell!"

Tom flicked the reins and they
made their way out of the village.

"We'll need a lot more than good
luck to stop Malvel," he heard Elenna
mutter at his back.

As though in response to Elenna's
words, the image of Malvel flickered
into sight in the air ahead of them,

the eyes flashing, the mouth twisted in an evil grin. Tom clutched his sword at the sight of the wizard, ready to fight again despite his exhaustion. But the vision was gone in an instant, leaving only the fading cackle of Petra's horrible laughter in their ears.

Tom relaxed his grip on his sword hilt. Elenna was right – they were a long way from defeating the wizard and his spiteful little helper.

Tom gritted his teeth with renewed determination – unless the wizard was defeated, their good friend Aduro would be lost forever. *No! I won't let that happen*. He dug his heels into Storm's side.

"Onwards!" he cried, as the stallion broke out into a gallop. Elenna gave a cheer. Their Quest hadn't ended yet, not by a long way.

Join Tom on the next stage
of the Beast Quest when he meets

KorakA
THE WINGED
ASSASSIN

Win an exclusive
Beast Quest T-shirt and goody bag!

Tom has battled many fearsome Beasts and we want to know which one is your favourite! Send us a drawing or painting of your favourite Beast and tell us in 30 words why you think it's the best.

Each month we will select **three** winners to receive a Beast Quest T-shirt and goody bag!

Send your entry on a postcard to
BEAST QUEST COMPETITION
Orchard Books, 338 Euston Road, London NW1 3BH.

Australian readers should email:
childrens.books@hachette.com.au

New Zealand readers should write to:
Beast Quest Competition, 4 Whetu Place, Mairangi Bay, Auckland NZ, or email: childrensbooks@hachette.co.nz

**Don't forget to include your name and address.
Only one entry per child.**

Good luck!

Join the Quest,
Join the Tribe

www.beastquest.co.uk

Have you checked out the Beast Quest website?
It's the place to go for games, downloads, activities,
sneak previews and lots of fun!

You can read all about your favourite Beasts, down-
load free screensavers and desktop wallpapers for
your computer, and even challenge your friends
to a Beast Tournament.

Sign up to the newsletter at www.beastquest.co.uk
to receive exclusive extra content and the oppor-
tunity to enter special members-only competitions.
We'll send you up-to-date info on all the Beast
Quest books, including the next exciting series
which features six brand-new Beasts!

Get 30% off all Beast Quest Books at www.beastquest.co.uk
Enter the code BEAST at the checkout.

Offer valid in UK and ROI, offer expires December 2013

All books priced at £4.99,
special bumper editions
priced at £5.99.

Orchard Books are available from all good bookshops, or can
be ordered from our website: www.orchardbooks.co.uk,
or telephone 01235 827702, or fax 01235 8227703.

FREE
COLLECTOR
CARDS
INSIDE!

Series 9: THE WARLOCK'S STAFF
COLLECT THEM ALL!

Malvel is up to his evil tricks again! The fate of
all the lands is in Tom's hands...

978 1 40831 316 9

978 1 40831 317 6

978 1 40831 318 3

978 1 40831 319 0

978 1 40831 320 6

978 1 40831 321 3

Series 10: Master of the Beasts
Out March 2012

Meet six terrifying new Beasts!

Noctila the Death Owl
Shamani the Raging Flame
Lustor the Acid Dart
Voltrex the Two-Headed Octopus
Tecton the Armour-Plated Giant
Doomskull the King of Fear

Watch out for the next Special Bumper Edition Grashkor the Death Guard! OUT JAN 2012!

978 1 40831 517 0

The Chronicles of Avantia

FROM THE DARK, A HERO ARISES...

Dare to enter the kingdom of Avantia.

A new evil arises in Avantia. Lord Derthsin has ordered his armies into the four corners of Avantia. If the four Beasts of Avantia can find their Chosen Riders they might have the strength to challenge Derthsin. But if they fail, the land of Avantia will be lost forever...

FIRST HERO, CHASING EVIL, CALL TO WAR, FIRE AND FURY OUT NOW!

www.chroniclesofavantia.com